Jo-Jo
the
Melon Donkey

This edition first published in Great Britain in 1999
First published in Great Britain 1995 by Mammoth
an imprint of Egmont Children's Books Limited
239 Kensington High Street, London W8 6SA.
Published in hardback by Heinemann Library,
a division of Reed Educational and Professional Publishing Limited
by arrangement with Egmont Children's Books Limited.
Text copyright © Michael Morpurgo 1995
Illustrations copyright © Tony Kerins 1995
Additional illustrations copyright © Tony Kerins
The Author and Illustrator have asserted their moral rights.
Paperback ISBN 0 7497 3581 3
Hardback ISBN 0 431 06189 0
10 9 8 7 6 5 4 3 2 1
A CIP catalogue record for this title
is available from the British Library.
Printed at Oriental Press Limited, Dubai.

MICHAEL MORPURGO

Jo-Jo
the
Melon Donkey

Illustrated by Tony Kerins

🍌 YELLOW BANANAS

Chapter One

JO-JO WAS A donkey. His father had been a donkey before him, and his mother as well. And so, of course, Jo-Jo had to be a donkey whether he liked it or not. And he did not like it, not one bit.

Work began early every morning for Jo-Jo. First, his master would load him with so many melons that he could hardly walk. Then he would drive him out of the village and down the dusty road towards the great city of Venice.

Jo-Jo loved Venice. It was his city. He loved the canals and the bridges, and the little squares and the sound of the church bells ringing out over the rooftops. He loved to stand and watch the water lapping around the houses, almost as if it wanted to suck the city back into the sea.

All day long his master would haul him down the narrow footpaths that ran alongside the canals, and Jo-Jo would call out, 'Melons. Melons. Melons for sale!' His braying would echo down the canals and into the squares. Everyone would know it was Jo-Jo, the melon donkey, and come running with their money. And all the while the flies came to torment him and would not go away,

Only in the cool of the evening resting under his olive tree, were there no flies to bother him and no master to bully him. Then at last he could be at peace. He would roll blissfully in his patch of dust, shake himself happy and lie down to dream.

Chapter Two

ONE MISTY SUMMER sunrise his master woke him as usual.

'Up, up, up, you old ragbag,' he shouted. 'No more little back streets for me. I'm going up in the world. I've heard they'll pay double for melons in St Mark's Square – that's where the rich folks live. Even the Doge, the ruler of Venice himself, might buy one of my melons.'

The load was even heavier that morning, but Jo-Jo didn't mind. He had a sudden feeling inside him that something good was about to happen.

By the time they reached St Mark's Square,
the sun was high in the sky and the square was
already full of people.

'Don't know why I never thought of this
before,' said his master, unloading the melons.

'This is the place for us, right in front of the
Cathedral. We'll sell them all in no time. Sing
out, you old ragbag you, sing out.'

'Melons. Melons. Melons for sale!' Jo-Jo
brayed, and his cry rang around the square.

Everyone in St Mark's Square stopped and turned and looked. And then one of them began to laugh, and then another and another until the entire square was filled with laughter.

'What are you laughing at?' asked Jo-Jo's master. 'You've seen a donkey before, haven't you? What's so funny?'

'Above your head,' they cried. 'Look above your head!' Jo-Jo and his master looked up. Behind them, glowing in the sun, stood the four golden horses of Venice, the four most beautiful horses in all the world. 'Beauty and the beast!' roared the crowd. 'Beauty and the beast.' Jo-Jo hung his head in shame.

All morning the people came to point and stare, but they bought no melons. 'Take your donkey to the back streets, where he belongs,' they said. 'And you can take your melons too. We don't eat melons here. They're not for the likes of us.'

Then, as noon chimed, the great doors of the Doge's Palace opened and a little girl ran out into St Mark's Square, a nurse bustling after her.

'Come back, come
back,' the nurse cried.
'You know you're not
allowed out of the
palace.'

'But I want a melon,' said the little girl. 'And
anyway I don't like being cooped up in that
palace all day. I've got no friends to play with
and I'm bored.'

'It's the Doge's daughter,' someone
whispered; and soon everyone was there,
bowing and curtseying as she passed. She
ignored them all and made straight for the pile
of melons beside Jo-Jo.

'How much do you want for one of your melons?' she asked Jo-Jo's master.

'Such an honour, Highness. Such an honour,' replied Jo-Jo's master. 'For Your Highness, it's a gift. I have the best melons in all of Venice, Highness, and this one is for you.'

'Thank you,' said the Doge's daughter, taking the melon; and then she noticed Jo-Jo standing beside his master.

'He has such sad, kind eyes,' she said. And she reached out and stroked Jo-Jo on his neck. Jo-Jo had never been patted in all his life, and his knees weakened with joy.

'Really, Your Highness,' said the nurse, taking the Doge's daughter by the arm. 'Fancy touching that filthy creature. Can't you see there are flies all over him? Come along back to the palace before your father sees you.' And she hustled the little girl away.

Jo-Jo closed his eyes and held the picture of the little girl in his mind so that it would never go away.

Within a few minutes all the melons were
sold. Suddenly anyone who was anyone in St
Mark's Square was eating melons. After all, what
was good enough for the Doge's daughter was
good enough for them.

So every day that summer, Jo-Jo came to
St Mark's Square loaded with melons and
stood under the four golden horses in front
of the Cathedral. And every day the Doge's
daughter came at noon for her melon. And
every time she came, she never failed to smile
at Jo-Jo. She would always talk gently to him
and smooth his nose before she left.

Chapter Three

ONE AFTERNOON, WHILE his master dozed under his hat and the whole city slumbered through the heat of the day, Jo-Jo was gazing up at the four shining golden horses in St Mark's Square, as he often did. They were everything the donkey longed to be but never could be.

'Oh, why can't I be like you?' he cried.

His master woke from his snoring sleep and beat him.

'How dare you wake me like that?' he roared.
'No use talking to those horses. Can't you see
they're nothing but statues? Statues can't hear.
Statues can't speak.'

But Jo-Jo knew they could.

The very next morning, just after Jo-Jo and his master arrived in the square, the Great Doge came to the window of his palace. Trumpets sounded and a crowd gathered to listen.

'Be it known to one and all,' said the Doge, 'that I intend to purchase the finest horse in the city for my daughter's birthday. A price of ten thousand ducats will be paid. The horse will be chosen at noon this very day, for today is my daughter's birthday. Let the bells ring out!'

All that morning Jo-Jo stood and watched the horses arriving in the square. Every one of them was finer than the one before and every one of them made him feel smaller and uglier than ever. There were black Arabian stallions with tossing heads, snorting as they came. There were grey Spanish mares with flowing manes, prancing as they came. Soon all the finest horses in the city were there, and a huge crowd had gathered.

As the noon bell sounded, the great Doge

came out into the square with his daughter, and the grand parade began. The crowd clapped and cheered as all the horses trotted by.

Then all of Venice waited silently to hear his choice.

'My daughter is ten years old today,' he said, 'so she is quite old enough to choose for herself.' He turned to his daughter.

'Now my child,' he said, 'which one would you like?'

The Doge's daughter walked slowly along the line of waiting horses, and then, at last she turned away and pointed. 'Over there!' she said, pointing towards the four golden horses.

'But you can't have them,' laughed the Doge, 'you can't have the golden horses. They belong to the people of Venice. They've been there for hundreds of years.'

'Not them,' the Doge's daughter said. 'I want that one over there, the one that's standing by the melons, Father.'

The crowd gasped.

'But that's a donkey! You want a donkey?' the Doge cried.

'Yes, Father,' said the Doge's daughter.

'I forbid it,' said the Doge, 'I absolutely forbid it. I cannot have a daughter of mine riding around on some flea-bitten donkey!'

'I don't want to ride around on him,' said the Doge's daughter. 'I want him to be my friend. I have no friends to play with, Father. You did say I could choose any one I wanted. And he's not flea-bitten at all. He's beautiful. He's much more beautiful than any of the others.'

'Don't you argue with me,' thundered the Doge. 'You could have picked the finest horse in the land and you chose that walking carpet. Look at him with his feet curled up like Turkish slippers!'

'Father,' said the Doge's daughter, her eyes filling with tears, 'if I cannot have the donkey I don't want anything.'

'All right,' said the Doge. 'If that's what you want then you will go without a present. Go back into the palace and go to your room at once.'

But the Doge's daughter ran across the square to where Jo-Jo stood and put her arms around his neck. 'Come to the palace tonight,' she whispered, 'and wait outside my window. I shall climb down and we shall run away together. Be there, Jo-Jo. Do not fail me.'

Whatever names they called Jo-Jo as his
master dragged him away through the crowds,
he did not mind. When they threw their melon
skins at him, he did not mind. For the first time
in his life, Jo-Jo was proud he was a donkey.

'Don't go getting any grand ideas inside that
ugly head of yours, you old ragbag,' his master
said. 'You're just a donkey, and a pretty poor
one at that, and don't forget it. Once a donkey,

always a donkey. And what's more you'll have
no supper tonight after what you've cost me.
If you'd have been a horse I'd be richer by ten
thousand ducats. Do you hear me?'

Jo-Jo heard him, but he was not listening. He
was making plans.

Chapter Four

JO-JO DID NOT sleep that night. He was too
excited. He waited until all was quiet and then
set to work. In the black of the night Jo-Jo bit
through the rope that tied him to his olive tree
and made his way carefully through the sleeping
village, down the road and back into the city of
Venice. It was a wild, wet and windy night. No
one heard Jo-Jo hurrying through the empty
streets, trotting over the little bridges, across St
Mark's Square towards the Doge's Palace.

In her bedroom in the palace, the Doge's daughter was waiting for Jo-Jo. When she heard him calling, she let herself down out of her window and ran over to him. 'Not so loud, Jo-Jo,' she said. 'You'll wake everyone up.'

And then she too heard the distant roar of the sea and heard the waves rolling in. She felt the

water round her ankles and understood why
Jo-Jo was braying. She knew at once what had
to be done.

With the Doge's daughter on his back, Jo-Jo
trotted braying through the city streets, waking
everyone up.

'What?' they shouted, opening their windows
and looking out into the dark streets. 'Melons at
this time of night?'

'No, no!' cried the Doge's daughter. 'The sea has broken in and the city is under water. Save yourselves!'

And all the while the sea came in, flooding the square and the Cathedral and the Doge's Palace itself. Woken by Jo-Jo's braying, the people of Venice ran for their lives.

Jo-Jo the melon donkey, with the Doge's daughter on his back, guided the children and the old people to safety down the flooding streets. And all the time the waters rose round them. Houses crumbled and the great bell tower in the square came crashing down into the water.

Chapter Five

WHEN MORNING CAME they discovered that not a single life had been lost. Jo-Jo, the melon donkey, had saved the people of Venice, and they loved him for it. It was the people who asked the Doge to put up a statue, a golden statue of the melon donkey. It should stand, they said, in St Mark's Square in front of the golden horses themselves, so that no one should ever forget him.

At the unveiling ceremony the Doge placed a laurel on Jo-Jo's head and apologised for the cruel things he had said about him. 'There is a legend,' the Doge said, 'that if ever the people of Venice were in danger, the four golden horses would save them. It's a nice story, but it's just a story. It was Jo-Jo the melon donkey who saved us and we must never forget it.'

And Jo-Jo smiled secretly inside himself and was happy.

Never again was Jo-Jo made to carry anything: except, that is, for the garlands of flowers that people put around his neck whenever he went out for a walk. For he became the Doge's daughter's donkey. And he was her friend and constant companion for the rest of his life. And donkeys do live for donkey's years, you know.

Yellow Bananas are bright, funny,
brilliantly imaginative stories written by
some of today's top writers. All the books
are beautifully illustrated in full colour.

**So if you've enjoyed this story, why
not pick another from the bunch?**

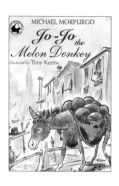